Scurvy Validation

Play

Scurvy Validation

Play

Oluwafunmilayo Inemesit Adewole

Soft Grid Limited

Oluwafunmilayo Inemesit Adewole

Published by

Soft Grid Limited

Plot 6, Block 23, Satellite Town

Calabar, Cross River, Nigeria

+234 (0)8027676550, +234 (0)8053110637

E-mail: softgridbooks@gmail.com

softgridltd@hotmail.com

www.softgridbookslimited.com

© Oluwafunmilayo Inemesit Adewole

First Published in 2020

ISBN 978-978-56095-8-5

Soft Grid Books

All Rights Reserved

First Printing, November 2020

Dedication

iii

To Almighty God for his loving-kindness, wisdom and tender mercies towards me. I also dedicate this to the best parents in the world, Mr and Mrs Adewole, for all their sacrifices and support to bringing out the best in me. Cheers to my wonderful siblings, Kofoworola and Mofiyin Adewole for always being there.

CHARACTERS

Anjola Adebayo

Mr Adebayo-   **Anjola's Father**

Mrs Adebayo-   **Anjola's Mother**

Eniola Ajayi-   **Awardee/Anjola's Classmate**

Oluchi Ulocha-   **Awardee/Anjola's Classmate**

Ewa-   **Anjola's Classmate**

Chiamaka-   **Anjola's Classmate**

Barakat-   **Anjola's Classmate**

Kitan Bello-   **Awardee/Anjola's Classmate**

Ore-   **Anjola's Classmate**

Kayode-   **SSS 3 Boy**

Senior Busayo-   **SSS 3 Girl**

Peju-   **Anjola's Classmate**

Abiola-   **Anjola's Classmate**

Azeem-   **Anjola's Classmate**

SCURVY VALIDATION

Nkechi-	Azeem's Friend
Kenneth-	Anjola's Classmate
Mr Olafare-	Teacher
Principal Victoria-	The Principal
Miss Dele-	House Mistress
Mrs Ezekiel-	Anjola's Class Teacher
Senior Folake-	SSS 1 Girl
Senior Ope-	SSS 3 Girl
Grace-	Anjola's Classmate
Mrs Olufemi-	Teacher
Mr Oyeniyi-	Teacher
Favour-	JSS 2 Girl
Motun-	JSS 2 Girl
Mr Thomas:	The Adebayo's Driver
External Invigilator	

SCURVY VALIDATION

ACT ONE

Scene I

It is a bright and beautiful day, which is perfect for Green College's on-going prize giving ceremony. The different shades of exquisite lighting and decorative materials make the newly white and gold painted walls more stunning and attractive. The atmosphere is full of jubilation as there are sounds of cheers, claps, songs from exotic musical instruments, along with the savory aroma from various dishes.

Mrs Olufemi: Our distinguished guests, esteemed parents, guardians, excellent teachers and indomitable students, it is with utmost pleasure I usher you into the next segment of our program.

Audience: (Claps and whistles.)

Mrs Olufemi: (Grins) We are about to call on the awardees. In few minutes, my colleague, Mr Oyeniyi will join me on stage. (Clears throat. Stands on the podium and reads out the awards for JSS 3 Class.) Best in English Language.

Mr Oyeniyi: (Joins Mrs Olufemi on the podium and calls out the names of the awardees) Oluchi Ulocha.

Mrs Olufemi: Best in French Language

Mr Oyeniyi: Oluchi Ulocha

Mrs Olufemi: Best in Home Economics

Mr Oyeniyi: Oluchi Ulocha

Oluchi Ulocha: (Jumps off seat and covers mouth with hands) Oh, my God, I was not expecting these much. (She approaches the podium cheerfully.)

Mr Oyeniyi: Can Mr and Mrs Ulocha join their daughter on the podium to receive the awards. Come up, Sir, Ma, it is a thing of pride.

Audience: (Claps continuously…)

Oluchi Ulocha: (Comes on podium with parents. Bobs and receives awards.)

(Crowd cheers as the photographers click their cameras around Oluchi. The round of applause thinly fades.)

Oluchi Ulocha: Foremost, I give thanks to Almighty God for this feat. I want to thank my teachers for imparting great knowledge, and I say a wonderful thank you to my parents who make the best provisions for my education. (Turns to parents.) Thank you mommy, thank you daddy, I really appreciate.

Audience: (Gives resounding round of applause.)

Mrs Olufemi: We will move on to the next award. (Clears throat and smiles.) Best in Mathematics.

Mr Oyeniyi: And he is… (Spreads an arm towards the audience.) Kitan Bello.

Mrs Olufemi: Best in Computer Science

Mr Oyeniyi: Kitan Bello

Mrs Olufemi: Best in Basic Science

Mr Oyeniyi: Kitan Bello

Kitan Bello: (Walks smartly to the podium with his mother.)

They receive the awards. The crowd cheers for him as he smiles for the camera.

Mrs Olufemi: The ceremony gets more interesting as we wind down to call it a great memorable day. The award for best student in Introduction to Technology goes to...

Mr Oyeniyi: Eniola Ajayi

Mrs Olufemi: Best in Agricultural Science

Mr Oyeniyi: Eniola Ajayi

Mrs Olufemi: Best in Social Studies

Mr Oyeniyi: Eniola Ajayi

Mrs Olufemi: Best in Yoruba Language

Mr Oyeniyi: Eniola Ajayi

Mrs Olufemi: Best in Christian Religious Knowledge

Mr Oyeniyi: Eniola Ajayi

Audience: (Cheer and clap in amazement) Eni, Eni, Eni, Eni, Eni!

(Light fades.)

In the car, Mrs Adebayo speaks to her daughter, Anjola.

Mrs Adebayo: (Stares intensely at Anjola) Anjola, I am not happy.

Anjola: (Sheepishly plays with finger and fearfully

stares at the steering wheel) I know, mommy. I am sorry.

Mrs Adebayo: (Head downcast. Breathes heavily and speaks sternly) They called you out on the podium for the best in. (Pauses and pretends to recall.) Please, remind me, dear. What was the award? (Looks up to Anjola and scowls.)

Anjola: (Shivers and bows) I do not understand. Are you mocking me?

Mrs Adebayo: Anjola, shut your mouth and give an answer to my question. They called you out for best in what. (Puts a hand on forehead.)

Anjola: (Crying) Nothing, mommy, nothing, they did not call me out…

Mrs Adebayo: (Yells) Exactly. Nothing, you are best in nothing. (Sighs and clasp hands.) The people that received awards, do they have two heads. You do not even have half an award to your name. For all the fees and time invested in your academics, all I got in return was a huge embarrassment. It is sad we pay expensive school fees for you to warm the school chair with your buttocks.

Anjola: (Cries and burrows head in-between thighs)

Mommy, I am sorry.

Mrs Adebayo: (Rolls eyes) What are you sorry? It is your life o.

Anjola: (Sniffs) Mommy, I promise to do better, I promise.

Mrs Adebayo: Please, do better. You have to do better because you have been an embarrassment. The school called us for a donation that was why I came; it is not that I wanted to clap for the awardees. And note that your father is furious. How can he come for this ceremony and his daughter is not a recipient of any award.

Anjola: Mommy, I will do better. Believe me. I am trying my best.

Mrs Adebayo: You need to try a lot harder. My patience is thinning. Those students that received awards are boarders, and you too are a boarder, so whatever they are doing to excel, make sure to surpass them. You have same opportunities but you have to be steps ahead, you have to study beyond your classrooms. Do you not have textbooks and library card?

Anjola: (Holds Mrs Adebayo's hands) Mommy, I

promise I will be more studious with my academics.

Mrs Adebayo: (Pats Anjola's hands) I believe you; I know you will make us proud, Anjola Adebayo. (Hugs Anjola) My dear, I just want the best for you. All I desire is to see you great like your peers and even greater.

Anjola: Soon, mommy, you will celebrate with me.

Mrs Adebayo: I know you can do it. All the best, let me know if you need anything. Your father and I are always available to give you the best.

Anjola: And I pray God keeps you and daddy in good health. I want to make both of you proud.

(They hug. Mrs Adebayo pecks Anjola on the cheeks.)

(Blackout.)

Scene II

The next day. In the hostel's courtyard. Miss Dele puts on her sneakers in readiness to do some morning workout. The girls are taking turns to do their toiletries. Busayo walks pass Miss Dele.

Senior Busayo: Good morning, Miss Dele.

Miss Dele: Good morning. (Stretching arms) Busayo, I want every corridor and staircases swept thoroughly. I will walk barefoot to ascertain the level of cleanliness. Let me not feel sand or any object on the floor. Take charge and let the girls carry out their duties with diligence.

Senior Busayo: Yes ma, (Bobs.)

(Light fades.)

An hour later. Miss Dele poses at the foot of the refectory's entrance. The students walk into the dining hall in groups. Miss Dele stops Busayo at the entrance.

Senior Busayo: (Stops and scowls) Miss Dele. (Stomach

grumbles.)

Miss Dele: I can see today is not your lucky day. You did not oversee the task I set out for your juniors.

Seniro Busayo: Ma, they did. I…

Miss Dele: They did not. And you will take up the broom and do it yourself.

Senior Busayo: But, ma, they…

Miss Dele: Off you go. Now!

Senior Busayo: (Storms off to the dormitory.)

(Busayo sweeps and says inaudible words while her stomach grumbles loudly.)

The boarding students of Green College are done with Saturday's breakfast and heads back to their hostels.

Miss Dele: JSS 3 girls, you want to hurry up with tidying the kitchen. You must be on time for morning preparatory session.

JSS 3: (Murmuring and exchanging heated words.)

Miss Dele: Who are those? What is the argument? Was that what I asked you girls to do?

JSS 3 Girls: (Murmur incoherent words.)

Miss Dele: Okay, carry on, the consequences awaits the initiators of this rouse. However, I want every chore completed. (Turns to Grace.) Grace, you are in charge.

Grace: (Bobs nervously) Yes, ma.

Miss Dele nods and leaves.

Peju: (Pours some liquid wash into a bowl of water) Here we go again. (Exhales.) I wonder why boys cannot wash plates in this school.

Grace: That one is a no go area; it is not negotiable in here. Since my entrance into this school, we have been complaining. (Waves a hand.) So, let us change the topic.

Peju: I know it is a waste of time arguing over that. I just wish for a revolution. Washing of dishes should not be an exclusive task for the females.

Grace: I hope that will change. I will like to see it happen before we graduate from this school. (Shakes head hopefully.) Where is Barakat? (Looks around the refectory.) She is not here. (Put hands on waist and wipes forehead with a face towel.) Seriously, girls, I do not understand. Do I have to get on my knees before she does her duty? A sluggish teammate is a bore.

Peju: (Washing plates) Hmmm, just call out to her. I saw her walking towards Senior Kayode.

Grace: Why should I go to her? You know she will be giving me attitude, as if she is the only one that has a school father. She had better come back soon, so that we can wash the dishes. I have greater things to do.

Peju: I do not think you do. If you are ready, you have to go after her. There is a need to do that because you get to accomplish your task whenever she washes the plates. You are to rinse the plates. (Laughs hysterically.)

Grace: (Sighs and walks out to call Barakat.)

Barakat: (Laughs and holds Kayode's hands) But Busayo said you started it all.

Kayode: Please tell her, to stop being dramatic and…

Grace: Good morning, Senior Kayode.

Kayode: (Responds without taking his eyes off Barakat) Good morning, Grace.

Grace:	(Irritatingly turns to Barakat) Barakat, I need your attention.
Barakat:	(Sighs and rolls eyes.)
Grace:	Barakat, come and wash the plates.
Barakat:	(Turns to Grace's direction with a repulsive look) Is that why you are shouting. Go, I am coming. As you can see, I am busy with my school father.
Grace:	(Appraises Barakat from head to feet) Please, we are mates o. You had better come and wash the plates. (Grumbles and walks away.)
Barakat:	(Waves off Grace and continues conversing with Kayode.)
Grace:	(Comes into the kitchen) Can you imagine that Barakat. (Claps hands in wonder.) I also have a school father and mother o. What is she feeling like? I mean, she is not even fine, with her nose like fertilized pepper.
Anjola:	(Approaches the kitchen hastily) I came for gist, what happened?
Peju:	(Rolls eyes at Anjola and continues to wash the plates.)

Anjola:	(Rolls eyes in excitement and claps hands) It must be interesting. Oh, Peju, I know that look.
Grace:	In fact, I will report this to Miss Dele, she will get what is coming for her.
Anjola:	(Laughs frenziedly.)
Oluchi:	(Walks in and drops broom) What happened? Why is Grace's face like this? (Feigns a shiver.) She really looks scary. Someone is going to be in a deep pot of hot soup. Who is the unlucky person, this time?
Barakat:	(Walks in quietly and begins washing plates.)
Anjola:	I thought I was the only one who noticed.
Oluchi:	Anjola, I hope you are getting ready for the tutorial.
Anjola:	(Smiles warmly) Yes, Oluchi. I am more than ready. Thanks for agreeing to be my tutor.
Oluchi:	You are welcome. Make sure to be on time.
Anjola:	Sure, I will be at your bunk by 2 pm, sharp.
Oluchi:	(Nods) Mathematics is first on the timetable.
ANJOLA:	That is my greatest challenge. (Shakes head.) I

do not comprehend the subject.

Oluchi: (Laughs) Do not worry. With dedication and hard work, all that would change.

Anjola: Hmmm, Oluchi, Oluchi. The all subjects' guru.

Oluchi: Why are you flattering me? (Laughs.) Please, put me down o. If I knew it all, my parents would not have bothered to pay more school fees.

Grace: (Yawns and rolls eyes) Are we here to solve our personal problems or to do the dishes.

Barakat: Look who is snooping on others.

Grace: Are you talking to me?

Peju: Oh, please, girls. Can you babes just stop? Did you both wake up from the wrong sides of your beds?

Oluchi: Grace, you like picking on people. Please, let us work in peace.

Grace: Oh, it is obvious there has been a gang up…

Barakat: Oh, please. (Continues to wash the dishes.)

Grace: I know what you girls are up to; I will just

pretend to be in the dark. (Rinses off the dishes.)

Oluchi: Who has your time? (Disposes dirt in the dustbin.)

(Loud Murmurings.)

Anjola: (Closes her ears over the incoherent banters.)

(The girls round up their chores. They argue all the way to the dormitory.)

(Light fades.)

Scene III

Miss Dele: JSS 3 girls, hurry up and come have your morning preparatory session. You need to be punctual at all times. It is just two months to your Examinations.

JSS3 Girls: (They chorus politely) Yes ma, we will.

The students assemble and sit in the school hall. They opened different notebooks and textbooks. Preparatory session commences with decorum and ends.

Senior Yetunde says the closing prayer after the preparatory sessions.

Senior Yetunde: Lord, please let us all pass our examinations in flying colours.

All Students: Amen!

Senior Busayo: (Picks up a microphone and quickly speaks before it gets rowdy) Room Pink girls, do not allow me to get to the dorm before you. (Carries her school bag and heads out.)

JSS 3 and SS1 students rush to the dormitory.

Senior Folake: (Drops her school bag on her bed) Girls, who swept today? (Looks from one girl to another with an aggressive posture.)

Senior Busayo: (Walks into the dormitory, gives Eniola Ajayi her bag.)

Eniola Ajayi: (Drops bag on Busayo's bed.) Let me confirm the names of those deployed to sweep. (Checks the roaster and turns to Grace.) She is the one. (Points at Grace.)

Senior Folake: Eh, so it is Grace's task to sweep today. Who is your partner (Checks roaster.) It is Chiamaka. Good, two of you, kneel in front of my bunk.

JS3-SS1 Girls: (Chatting indistinctly.)

Senior Busayo: (Heads to locker and picks a red hanger) Can you imagine I swept for my juniors. Are you girls in JSS1 that I should be looking at how you sweep. (Beats Chiamaka and Grace on their backs with the red hanger.)

Senior Folake: Wow! (Laughs as she climbs on Busayo's bed) Busayo, you were merciless with that hanger o.

Senior Busayo: Miss Dele did not only make me sweep for my junior, she also questioned my capabilities as a senior girl and school prefect. She asked me if I know what I am doing. She mocked my role as the Head of Labour. (Sighs.)

Senior Ope: (Laughs) Thank God I went to the sickbay, because, I would have dealt with you people. What Senior Busayo has done is nothing compared to what I would do.

Senior Busayo: Ope, it was not funny. I swept for these girls. My sweat soaked my uniform and I could not go to the refectory looking like a drenched puppy. Their incompetency made me missed my yummy noodles, today. (Rolls eyes.) Now, I want answers. Who was to sweep the staircase?

Chiamaka: (Looks at her feet) It was my duty to sweep that area, but Grace said she would do it. So, I went on to sweep the hostel corridor.

Senior Busayo: So, I swept on your behalf. Very Good, Chiamaka you can go. (Angrily advances on Grace.) You…

Motun: Senior Busayo, please, I have menstrual cramps.

Senior Busayo: (Stops and looks calmly at Motun) Have you Eaten?

Motun: (Holds midsection and shakes head slowly) No.

Senior Busayo:	Okay, sorry dear. Tell Eniola to give you cornflakes and come back for drugs.
Motun:	Thank you.
Senior Busayo:	If it were to embarrass somebody in the dining hall, you would open your dirty mouth.
Grace:	(Maliciously stares at Barakat.)
Barakat:	(Sits on Senior Busayo's bed and smirks.)
Senior Busayo:	Hey, look at me. I am talking to you. (Stares disgustingly.) For the next two weeks, you are to sweep this dormitory alone. (Turns around.) I hope everyone has heard. Grace is sweeping the dormitory alone for the next two weeks. (Stands in front of Grace.) Is my instruction clear?
Grace:	Yes, Senior Busayo.
Seniro Busayo:	Good, I hate to repeat myself. Now, get out of my sight. (Everyone begins to talk at once.) Keep quite. Silence, please…

(The murmuring gradually subsides.)

(Light fades.)

Light comes up on stage. Oluchi is alone in the library. The wall clock clanks to announce 2 pm. Oluchi looks at her wristwatch and stares at the library's door. Anjola has not come for the tutorial session. Oluchi begins to read. After thirty minutes, she sleeps on the book. She wakes and checks the time. She scrambles to her feet and runs off to the hostel in melancholy.

The same day. In the evening. Chiamaka and Anjola are having a conversation on their beds.

Chiamaka: Nawa o. (Sighs and whispers) Peju said, when Grace came upstairs during PREP to get her Maths textbook, Miss Dele snapped and told her to pick up the book and disappear from the dorm.

Anjola: (Moves closer and whispers) What do you mean?

Chiamaka: It is obvious, Barakat reported Grace to Miss Dele.

Anjola: Report on what?

Chiamaka: About who to wash and rinse off the plates. Did you not notice that Miss Dele has been picking on Grace? Whatever task meant for Barakat, Miss Dele asked Grace to get it done.

Anjola: You do not mean it. To think Grace wanted to report Barakat to Miss Dele. How did the table

	turn? (Shakes head.) Well, that is one of the advantages of having a school mother. Everyone knows Miss Dele is quite fond of Senior Busayo.
Chiamaka:	Oh, please, that is not an excuse. Barakat is wicked, why did she not wash the plates on time?
Anjola:	Abi, hmmm, she always has to feel like a Queen.
Chiamaka:	So, who is her slave in a school everybody pays the same fee.
Anjola:	That is unfair treatment from Miss Dele o.
Chiamaka:	I pity Barakat, Senior Busayo would graduate, all the seniors will beat and send her on plenty errands.
Anjola:	Eh, you do not know what you are saying. (Laughs) Barakat that already has Senior Folake and Senior Busayo as school mothers, and Senior Kayode as school father. I think that girl has her generation covered from ever doing chores like other students. It seems she has bewitched everybody in this school, from teaching to non-teaching staffs, and to the students.

Chiamaka: (Shrugs and sighs deeply) That one is her business. Secondary school is not the end of the world. She cannot escape commitment to hard work, unless, she does not have plans to be successful beyond this petty lane she is threading in this school.

Anjola: (Laughs) You are right. (Yawns.)

Chiamaka: Anjola, it is time to sleep. (Whispers.) We do not want the housemistress to catch us. Being a scapegoat is not nice.

Anjola: (Nods and closes eyes.)

Chiamaka: (Whispers) Good night, Anjola.

Anjola: (Snores softly.)

(Light fades.)

ACT TWO

Scene I

JSS 3 students are writing Junior WAEC. Some external invigilators supervise the students with the help of some teachers of Green College.

External Invigilator: (Walks gently around the school hall. He checks his wristwatch) You have three minutes more.

(There is loud murmuring and sound of feet movement.)

Oluchi: (Murmurs and writes swiftly.)

External Invigilator: Cross your 't' and dot your 'I' if need be.

Anjola: (Writing) Please sir, is there an extra time.

External Invigilator: (Turns swiftly to Anjola) Quiet!

Anjola: (Shudders and stops writing.) I am sorry. (Quickly ticks the answers on the objective examination paper.)

External Invigilator: This is an examination. As you can see, the examination is for two hours. Shade the answers you know is correct and move on. If you do not know the answers, submit your paper and prepare for the next paper. (Checks wristwatch.) Time's up, pass your papers forward. (Briskly moves to the front desk.)

(Students move in droves to submit examination papers in front of the External Invigilator.)

External Invigilator: (Collects and counts the answer booklets) Prepare for the next examination, all the best.

(The external invigilator leaves the hall as the students dismisses.)

(Light fades.)

After the examination, the school becomes rowdy. Day students leave for their various homes and boarders go to the hostels.

Anjola looks around for Barakat in the school. She bumps into Ewa.

Anjola: (Holds Ewa from falling) Oh, sorry, Ewa.

Ewa: (Catching her breath.)

Anjola: Have you perhaps seen Barakat? I have been looking all over for her.

Ewa: Eh, I think she went to the buttery.

Anjola: (Claps hands excitedly) Thank you. (Heads to the buttery.)

Ewa: (Sighs and walks towards Ore) Is it by force to be somebody's friend.

Ore: (Laughs) Don't be cheeky. She was just looking for Barakat.

Ewa: (Rolls eyes) Oh, please, it is obvious Anjola and Barakat are not on the same level. Why is she trying to glue her body to Barakat's clique? It is more annoying because Barakat does not like her.

Ore: (Laughs) That is a sad truth. Well, she can do whatever she pleases. It is not my business. Or is it any of your business what she chooses to do with her time and wits?

Ewa: It can never be my business.

Ore: I thought as much. Come on; let us be on our way.

Anjola: (Comes into the buttery) Ewa told me I would find Barakat, but I cannot see her anywhere.

(Looks around.) Where is Barakat? (Walks towards some students.) I will just ask some people. (Stands in front of some girls.) Hello, (Looks over their shoulders and sees Barakat with Oluchi and Eniola.) Oh, there they are. (Walks towards them and excitedly joins the conversation.)

Anjola: Hello girls. Barakat, you do not know for how long I have been looking for you. I am glad I found you. I was getting tired of the search.

Barakat: So, to what do I hold this successful discovery?

Anjola: What?

Barakat: Now that you found me, how may I help you?

Oluchi: (Laughs) Ah, Barakat, you are a yeye girl. Are you girls quarrelling?

Anjola: I wonder o. Oluchi, you noticed the way she is being cold towards me, right? If I tell you I understand Barakat, then I am a big lair.

Barakat: (Remorseful) I am sorry for being harsh. It was the stress of the examination. It was quite a tough exercise.

Anjola:	It is all right. How were your exams?
Barakat:	Ah, it was interesting. (Grins) Oluchi thank you. Your answers gave me a booster to do some by myself.
Oluchi:	(Beams) you are welcome.
Anjola:	You said what? Oluchi gave you answers to the questions.
Barakat:	How will a saint do that? Have you forgotten Oluchi is a serious Christian girl? (Giggles.)
Oluchi:	(Smiles coyly) Aha, but all of us are Christians.
Anjola:	Quit joking and tell me what went down at the examination hall. (Scratches her ears.) My eardrums are itching.
Barakat:	(Clears throat) Okay ma, there is not much to say. The gist is, Oluchi had explained the Basic Science to me.
Anjola:	(Jaws drop) Are you serious, and you did not call me. Barakat, you should have tagged me. You girls are not being fair to me. Oluchi, I was counting on you.
Barakat:	Well, I did not know you were interested.

Besides, if you were keen on preparing for the exam, you should have made yourself available. Who do you think has the time to force you to read? Did your parents pay school fees to Barakat? (Hisses.)

Anjola: (Puts a hand on her chin) Hmmm, Barakat, I thought we were friends.

Barakat: All right, my friend. (Put hands on Anjola's shoulders.) Okay, I am sorry, next time I will call you to read your books. (Laughs mockingly.)

Anjola: It is all right. Since Oluchi tutored you, it is best I take tutorials from her. Oluchi, what time should I come; I need serious lessons on French.

Oluchi: (Flares in annoyance) Time for what. I do not have time to waste. The era of persuading you to join my study class is over. You stood me up the last time, remember? I waited for you on my bunk like a fool. You did not even render an apology. (Removes eyeglasses and wipes face.) I will not include you in my reading group. You will slow us down. I cannot take any chances. Ask Eniola Ajayi, if she can help you.

Eniola: (Laughs) What do I know? Grace is teaching me French, and we are already a crowd in her group.

Anjola: Okay girls, thank you all for your honest contributions. (Walks away.)

Barakat: (Looks from Oluchi to Eniola.)

Eniola: Where are you going? Come on, Anjola. It is not enough to get angry at us.

Oluchi: (Laughs mockingly) Who says she is angry. Did you not hear when she thanked us?

Anjola: (Quickens her steps.)

Barakat: Adieu, my friend. (Burst into laughter.)

Oluchi: Barakat, are you saying goodbye for real to Anjola.

Barakat: Yes, it is good riddance to bad rubbish. That girl is way out of my league. I cannot tolerate her presence and interference any more. (Hisses.)

Eniola: Hmmm, I do not think that is a good decision. That girl is always at your disposal. Girls like Anjola are hard to come by in this school.

Barakat: (In deep thoughts) You are right, that girl is good for an emotional fool and domestic hand. I will just keep her on my fingertips; she comes in handy on some hard days.

Oluchi: Now you have on your thinking cap.

(The girls clap hands and exit the buttery.)

(Light Fades.)

In the dormitory. Light shines on Oluchi sitting sadly on her bunk.

Oluchi: I was really mean to Anjola. I wonder what got into me. I will have to apologise to her. I must. (Lies down.) I hope I see her tomorrow. What I did weighs heavily in my heart. (Toss and turns.)

(Light fades on Oluchi's sad countenance.)

Scene II

A week later. Assembly Ground in Green College.

Students: Green College shall live forevermore.

Principal Victoria: (Approaches podium with a microphone) Good morning students.

Students: Good morning, ma.

Principal Victoria: (Smiles and looks around) It is a beautiful morning, and I am pleased to see all my students happy and excited as we call forth an end to another term in the 2019/2020 session.

Students: (Claps and whistles.)

Principal Victoria: According to the school's calendar, today is our Open day/Vacation day. I know many of you have packed your bags before proceeding to the assembly ground. Therefore, I request you all be on your best conducts as we expect your parents and guardians. They shall comb through your academic performances through the term, and receive your report cards. Do not have hopes of getting your results if you are yet to complete the payment of your school fees.

Student: (Raises a hand) Excuse me, ma. I will like to ask a question.

Principal Victoria: I will not entertain any question on the assembly ground. For any complaint or other issues, your parents and guardians will convey it to me. In the absence of any related issue, we will dismiss the assembly. Happy Holidays!

Students: (Goes up in excited uproar.) Yeah, we love holidays!

Principal Victoria: (Laughs and clears throat) Hold on, lest I forget, there will be a short meeting with the prefects after the assembly. Please, move into your classrooms in an orderly manner.

(Light fades.)

The school's courtyard. Anjola is in a hurry to get her hanger from the cloth line. Abiola bumps into Anjola.

Anjola: (Rubs her forehead) You stupid girl, are you

blind or something.

Abiola: I am sorry, I was not watching. And you should not have been so fast to insult me. You owe me an apology.

Anjola: Did you say an apology. Now you are going to cause me a severe headache. You had better watch where you are going. (Looks at feet) Gosh, you even stepped on my shoe. What is wrong with you? (Grunts.)

Abiola: Oh, I am sorry, I did not mean to…

Peju: (Hisses and takes Abiola's arm) Abiola, that is enough apology in one day. And Anjola, all these rudeness you are imitating from Barakat does not suit you one bit. (Puts a hand on her waist and snap fingers.)

Anjola: Are you all right? (Frowns and gazes at Peju.)

Peju: Shut your mouth, why are you unnecessarily rude?

Anjola: Peju, I was not even talking to you. It is obvious you are such a busy body.

Abiola: You are indeed a fake drama queen. You always feel like you are very important because you are with someone who is as lousy, and does not care if you exist or in extinction. You are just a simpleton who is good at being a maid.

Anjola: (Bites a finger and shakes head) Hmmm, I do not know why I am talking to people like you. (Grabs hanger and walks away.)

Abiola: There she goes like a coward she is. I am so mad at myself for wasting my precious apologies.

(Abiola and Peju clap hands and laugh at Anjola.)

(Light fades.)

Light Shines Downstage.

Anjola: (Goes behind the hostel and sobs) Peju and Abiola were right. I am just a plaything to Barakat. (Sniffs.) It is just a matter of time; everyone would like and respect me. (Wipes tears.)

Barakat: (Walks towards Anjola) Hey Anjola, I was on the lookout for you. Here. (Brings out a wrapped item from her bag.) This is for you.

Anjola: Wow, (Takes the gift.) This is for me. (Tears the gift-wrap.) It is a perfume. (Hugs Barakat.) Thanks so much.

Barakat: You are welcome. I am sorry about the way I spoke to you.

Anjola: It is okay. I really appreciate this. And I feel awful that I do not have a gift to give to you.

Barakat: We have a resumption date. Remember that.

Anjola: Yeah, thanks, my friend.

Favour: (Walks towards Anjola and Barakat) Excuse me. Senior Anjola, your driver is here.

Anjola: Okay, Barakat. It is time for me to go. Favour. (Points at luggage.) Please, take my box and bucket to the gates for me.

Barakat: Have a lovely holiday. (Waves vigorously.) Bye. (Walks towards the hostel.)

Favour: Okay, Senior Anjola. (Picks up the bucket and wheels the box on the ground.)

Anjola: (Smiles) Peju and Abiola are so wrong. Barakat is a true friend. To think I took their spiteful words to heart. (Holds the gift to her heart.) Barakat, I am sorry for doubting your friendship. (Waves at Barakat's retreating figure.)

(Lights fades.)

Scene III

The Adebayo's Residence.

Mrs Adedayo: (Walks into Anjola's room) She is still asleep. Anjola, Anjola wake up.

Anjola: (Toss and turns.)

Mrs Adebayo: Anjola, I said wake. (Spanks her buttocks.)

Anjola: Ouch…Oh, mommy. (Rubs buttocks and sits.) Good morning, mommy.

Mrs Adedayo: Good morning. Snap out of the sleepiness and get about your chores. The sun is setting. Your laziness is getting extreme. (Leaves.)

Anjola: (Scratches eyes and yawns loudly) Someone cannot enjoy her sweet dreams in peace. Must all mornings be a chore day? There is no moment of rest in this house. If it is not sweeping, it is mopping the whole house. One day, my parents will ask me to sweep the neighbourhood because they just delight in stressing. (Hisses.)

MRS ADEBAYO: (Calls out) Anjola, you will not like what I

would do to you if I come back and meet you sleeping.

Anjola: (Stands and walks unsteadily to the kitchen) With the numerous house cleaners, we have, I wonder why I have to pick a pin.

(Light fades on Anjola washing plates and grumbling.)

The Adebayo's are having dinner. Mrs Adebayo's phone rings. She drops her cutleries and answers the call.

Mrs Adebayo: (On phone) Hello, good morning. (She listens and her pupils widened.) Oh, my Goodness.

Anjola: (Gives Mrs Adebayo a questioning stare.)

Mrs Adebayo: (Looks sadly at Anjola.) My condolence to the family, I will be there. (Hangs call.) That was a call from your school's Admin.

Anjola: (Eats slowly and wonders what is going on.)

Mrs Adebayo: Jesus, I cannot believe it.

Anjola: Mommy, what happened? (Stops eating and moves her plate aside.)

Mrs Adebayo: That intelligent girl in your school. What is her name again? (Snaps finger.) Eniola Ajayi, she died this morning.

Anjola: (Horrified) What?

Mrs Adebayo: My God. (Looks down and cries.)

Anjola: Mommy, who told you that?

Mrs Adebayo: Your school, the Admin just informed me. I am sorry, Anjola.

Anjola: I do not understand. Eniola is dead. I have to be dreaming. (Slaps cheeks.) She was near perfect. God, why did you take her? Jesus Christ! Is this how life is?

Mrs Adebayo: (Leaves seat and comes to Anjola.) This must be hard on you, Anjola. Please, accept my heartfelt condolences. (Pats Anjola's back.) The burial is on Saturday, we will be going to support and console her family.

Anjola: (Tears rolls down cheeks.) I wish you could tell me this is not happening.

Mrs Adebayo: I wish I could question God's will. (Sighs heavily and stops a tear from sliding down eyes.) I will get desert. (Leaves the dining table.)

(Anjola wipes her tears and sniffs into her

dress. She checks her phone and sees notification of the school's group chat. Many students are expressing their shock over Eniola's death. She leaves the dining table and nearly stumbles.)

Mrs Adebayo: (Holds Anjola's elbow) Watch it, Anjola. You could hurt yourself. Come sit at the dinning. Desert will be ready in two minutes.

Anjola: No, mommy, I am not interested. I have lost my appetite. (Runs away.)

(Light Fades.)

Scene IV

On Saturday. Family, friends and some members of Green School management are at the Ajayi's residence. Some adults console Mr and Mrs Ajayi. Anjola and some of her classmates are sitting in the second parlour.

Oluchi: (Frowns at some girls and boys taking pictures) Some people just came here to get selfies for social media vibes. Goodness gracious, we lost someone very precious to us. But look at them catching fun. Afterwards, I am sure they will shed some few crocodile tears.

Ewa: I am just feeling dispirited. I cannot explain.

Anjola: Why do I feel like she does not deserve to be the one to die?

Peju: No one deserves to die. But everyone must die. Nobody will live forever.

Kitan: All of a sudden, I feel being so serious in school is waste of time, I mean, look at Eniola. With all those awards, she is nowhere today.

Oluchi: (Shakes head) The universe did not allow her to shine at all.

Kitan: (Wrap hands over his arms) So unfair.

Anjola: (Cringes) Life is very unfair.

Peju: I just think, this life is very unpredictable and we should try living it to the fullest in every way positive.

Ewa: Eniola enjoyed schoolwork, so to me, she lived a fulfilled life.

Kayode: She made everyone proud and that is what everyone will remember of her.

Anjola: (In an aside) If I die today, what memory of me will people have? I am just empty.

Ewa: I am going to miss her so much.

Kitan: All of us will.

(Blackout.)

ACT THREE

Scene I

Green College Assembly ground. The old students are assessing some new students with inquisitiveness amidst whispers. Mr Oyeniyi directs the new students to stay on the line of their various classes. Azeem follows Mr Oyeniyi's instruction and positions himself amongst the SS 1 boys. Some SS 1 girls giggle over having a new male face in their set.

Principal Victoria: Welcome back, students of Green College. I trust you had a wonderful holiday.

Students: (Chorus) Yes ma.

Principal Victoria: It is a new beginning where we can choose to win again, or lose. But, my prayer and joy would be that all my students become winners. Listen, boys and girls. I am sincerely hurt when some of you underperform in your academics. It is definitely not, what our motto represents. We are here to groom excellent students that are sound in academics and morals. I want you all to dream big. Create great visions on the paths you want to lead in life and make it happen by winning at this stage. Am I making some sense?

Students: Yes ma. Thank you, ma.

Principal Victoria: (Smiles beautifully) SS 1 students.

SSS 1 Students: (Screams in excitement.)

Principal Victoria: How does it feel to be in senior uniform?

SSS 1 Students: (Screams in excitement) Great!

Principal Victoria: (Beams) SS 3 students, congratulations, you have reached the last lap of this journey. I see you all in greater heights.

SSS 3 Students: (Whistles) We are the graduating class!

Principal Victoria: (Laughs softly) You will all graduate in flying colours. Amen.

SSS 3 Students: Thank you, ma.

Principal Victoria: Our dear students, it is a new session, make the best out of it. God bless you all. Let us get to our classes in marching order. Bands!

The drummers begin to play their various instruments. The students march towards their classes in muffled chatters.

(Light fades.)

Mr Olafare addresses the entire student in SSS 1.

Mr Olafare: Good day, students. For those of you meeting me for the first time, I am Mr Olafare, and I am here to give guides on how to choose career paths. Once again, congratulations on advancing into the first phase of senior class.

SSS 1 Students: Thank you, sir.

Mr Olafare: Let me add that, you need to know your passion, strength, and weakness in all your subjects, because it will determine if you will be in Art, Commercial, or Science class. According to your Junior WAEC result, the school already knows the class you belong, but your choice is our command. We would like you to go into a class that interests you. Do not make decisions under peer pressure. Do not make a decision because the boy or girl you fancy is there.

SSS 1 Students: (Blushes and murmur.)

Mr Olafare:	(Tightens jaw) Murmur all you want, that is what some of you intend. I am only begging you, to refrain from such actions and thoughts. (Wave both hands.) I wish you all the best. I have faith; you will make this school proud. Excuse me for three minutes. (Takes phone from his pocket.)
Anjola:	(Catches the intense stare of Azeem. Coughs and adjusts her skirt and shirt.) Why is he staring? (Looks behind.) I could be mistaken; perhaps he is looking at someone else or just staring into space. (She turns to Barakat.) Barakat, you people did not even chill a bit, you slim fitted your school uniform on the first day.
Barakat:	(Winks) What do you expect from trendy boys and girls. The real deal is, let noting catch you un-fresh. (Anjola and Barakat giggles.)
Mr Olafare:	(Ends call) May I know why the two of you are laughing? Did I say something funny?
Anjola:	(Bows) No, sir. It was nothing funny. I was just…

Barakat:	(Laughter escapes her lips.)

Mr Olafare: Okay, that is it. (Inserts phone in pocket.) The both of you should get on your knees. Raise your hands and close your eyes. You know me. Failure to do what I have asked properly will cost you both more severe punishments.

(Barakat and Anjola serve the punishment in front of the class.)

Anjola: (Speaks softly) How did I get here. (Catches Azeem's stare.) What does this boy keep looking at? Is my skirt torn? (Scrutinizes skirt.) There is nothing wrong with my uniform. (Scowls at Azeem.)

(Light fades.)

The same day. Azeem is having a conversation with Kenneth.

Azeem: (Points at Anjola) See that girl siting at the edge of the last table.

Kenneth: (Looks in Anjola's direction) Yeah, that is Anjola.

Azeem: Hmmm, Anjola. (Rubs chin.) That is a pretty name for a beautiful girl.

Kenneth:	(Winks) Hmmm, I know that look from a dude portrays interest towards a girl.
Azeem:	(Smirks) Yeah, you know too much.
Kenneth:	(Smiles and drinks water from a bottle) Azeem, you just got into this school and you have already set your goal on a babe.
Azeem:	(Chuckles) Not just a babe, my heart is set on that girl. Is she single?
Kenneth:	(Nods) Yeah.
Azeem:	(Grins) Thank goodness. That means I have a chance of pursuing her.
Kenneth:	Should I introduce you to her?
Azeem:	(Holds Kenneth's shoulder) No, I got this.
Kenneth:	I hope you have great toasting skills up your sleeves.

(Lights Fades.)

Scene II

The next day. Break time. In the staff room. Anjola confusingly walks towards Mr Olafare's desk. She bobs and accepts the form he hands to her. She moves over to an empty desk.

Anjola: (Gawks at the registration form) How can I achieve this goal of being a medical practitioner when I failed Maths in my Junior WAEC. (Chews pen.) People would think I am a dullard if I choose any other class. Medicine has much professional recognition. I want to be in Science class because the happening people will be there. Barakat is going for Science. (Sighs and ticks Science class.) This will keep me in Barakat's circle. (Smiles satisfactorily.) I will have some recognition and feel amongst the big girls in her clique. (Submits form and goes out.)

(Oluchi and Chiamaka are anxiously waiting in the hostel's courtyard.)

Oluchi: Anjola, which of the classes did you choose.

Anjola:	Science class.
Chiamaka:	Wow, me too.
Oluchi:	That is great. Wow, you girls are going to be the doctors and lab people. I chose to be in Commercial class.
Anjola:	It is expected. You have always been a business-minded girl. Well, I will not miss you much, because I have Barakat and Grace in my class.
Oluchi:	What did you say?
Chiamaka:	(Raises a hand in Anjola's face) Hold on a minute. Who told you Barakat chose Science?
Anjola:	She told me she was opting for Science class, that she loves it with so much passion.
Oluchi:	Well, breaking news, Miss Anjola Adebayo. Barakat is in the same class as me. (Smirks.)
Anjola:	But she told me Science was her first and last choice, she…
Oluchi:	Anjola, I hope you did not tick Science class based on Barakat's choice.
Chiamaka:	(Stares in shock at Oluchi.) No, she did not.

Anjola:	I, I…
Oluchi:	(Turns to Anjola) Anjola, wow, you disappoint me. Despite the counsels from Mr Olafare, you went ahead to choose a career path based on someone's personal choices? (Holds head with both hands.) This is incredible. I am disappointed. (Walks away.)
Anjola:	Oluchi, wait, I…
Chiamaka:	Girl, you really fucked up. I wonder if Barakat has exchanged your head with that of a goat's head. (Hisses and walks away.)
Anjola:	(Tears rolls down cheeks) Anjola Adebayo, when will you stop being a fool.
Barakat:	(Walks towards Anjola) Hey, my wonderful friend. I guess you have made the big decision. There will be a little party at my bunk, just few candies and…
Anjola:	Barakat that is enough. (Wipes tears.) I have had enough of your fake friendship. I have been a fool. (Sniffs.) Now, I am a bit wiser.
Barakat:	Anjola, it is me your friend. Why the sudden change?
Anjola:	(Sniffs) Goodbye. (Walks away.)

Barakat:	(Mocking laughter) She is indeed a fool. (Claps hands.) She wants I, Barakat, to be in the same class with her. Thank goodness, she is out of my life. (Takes a deep breath.) I hope it is for good. (Fans her face with a hand and exhales.)

(Light fades.)

Later that same day. Anjola goes to Oluchi's bunk.

Anjola:	Oluchi.
Oluchi:	(Turns to the other side of her bunk) Please, I have no interest in speaking to you.
Anjola:	Oluchi, please, here me out. I am sorry for every dumb way I have acted. I need you now more than ever.
Oluchi:	If I may ask, how may I be of help to you?
Anjola:	(Wriggles hands) Help with my academics.
Oluchi:	(Sighs and sits) Anjola, I would have loved to help. But you have made that difficult by choosing a different class. It would be difficult to interchange subjects.
Anjola:	Please, Oluchi, you have to help me. No

knowledge is a waste. I know you can do it. And I promise to be your good student. I will listen to every good thing you tell me.

Oluchi:	(Stares hard at Anjola.)

Anjola:	(Bows and holds her breath.)

Oluchi:	I will sleep over it. Expect a response by tomorrow afternoon.

Anjola:	Thanks. (Smiles sadly.)

(Light fades.)

Later in the evening. (Light shines on Anjola shredding a friendship card. She takes out a gift item and dumps it in the dustbin.)

(Blackout.)

Scene III

Azeem sees Anjola walking down the corridor and he pretends to read a storybook.

Anjola: (Pauses) Is he stalking me? (Haughtily walks pass Azeem.)

Azeem: Hi, Anjola.

Anjola: (Flushes in excitement) He knows my name. (Bats eyelashes.)

Azeem: If you have few minutes to spare, I would like to talk to you.

Anjola: You are already talking to me.

Azeem: You are not speaking to me.

Anjola: The minutes are ticking.

Azeem: Okay, I will go straight to the point.

Anjola: Okay.

Azeem: I want you to be my girlfriend.

Anjola: (Blushes and runs to her classroom.)

Azeem: (Shakes head) This might not be easy. I need a backup.

(Light fades.)

In the classroom.

Anjola: (Closes Mathematics textbook) Oh, Oluchi, thank you so much.

Oluchi: You are welcome, Anjola. It is magical how you caught up with solving equations. Hmmm, I think there has been a genius lurking in your brain, you were just carried away to explore it.

Anjola: (Grins) I have you to thank for that, you are awakening the best in me. I am glad you gave me another chance.

Oluchi: It is all right, girl. I am always here for you. (Stretches an opened palm towards Anjola.)

Anjola: (Places a hand in Oluchi's palm.)

Oluchi: You can always count on me.

Anjola: (Grips Oluchi's hand) Thank you so much.

(Light fades.)

Light shines on classroom's corridor. Kenneth signals Azeem on Anjola's emergence.

Azeem:	(Quickly adjusts his belt and combs his hair.)
Anjola:	(Walks fast on seeing Azeem.)
Azeem:	(Runs after Anjola) Babe, hey, what is with the haste? I have been meaning to talk to you for a while.
Anjola:	(Stops abruptly.)
Azeem:	(Bumps into Anjola) I am so sorry.
Anjola:	Ouch. (Rubs her shoulder.) Now you have my attention.
Azeem:	I really like you. Please, accept me as your boyfriend.
Anjola:	I will…
Azeem:	(Places a finger on her lips) Please, do not say no. What is the harm? We will just be friends.
Anjola:	(Darts eyes around the corridor and sees a teacher.)
Azeem:	Please, be my girlfriend.
Anjola:	(Nods and darts eyeballs.)
Azeem:	Is that a yes?
Anjola:	(Nods desperately.)

Azeem:	(Removes finger) Yes, thanks baby. I will cherish you…
Anjola:	Hey listen, I nodded because….
Azeem:	(Runs off in excitement.)
Anjola:	Hey, come back. I might have agreed to be your girlfriend because I did not want the teacher to see us in such a compromised position. (Sighs and sluggishly walks towards the library.)

(Light fades.)

In the library. Anjola flashes back to her encounter with Azeem.

Anjola:	Maybe I should just date him. As he said, there is really no harm in us dating. (Rests chin on her hands.) That the new boy in school is asking me out is a big deal. Hmmm, I bet other girls will envy me. (Smiles.) Anjola now has a boyfriend.

(Oluchi enters the library.)

Oluchi:	Hmmm, I see someone is daydreaming.
Anjola:	(Quickly snaps out of her fantasy.)
Oluchi:	I see someone now has a boyfriend.
Anjola:	(Blushes.)

Oluchi: I saw the two of you.

Anjola: (Looks shocked) Did you?

Oluchi: I saw the last part. Just be careful, girl. And do not lose focus on your studies. Play very safe with that new boy.

Anjola: (Looks shy.)

Oluchi: Let us get down to business. It is not wise to dwell much on boys. (Opens Anjola's note.) Did you encounter any problem?

Anjola: Yes, please. See, these. (Shows some difficult equations.)

(Light fades on Anjola and Oluchi doing some revisions.)

Light shine downstage. Anjola and Azeem are in each other's company most of the time. Whenever they are in public gatherings, they cannot take their eyes off each other. Their relationship blossoms from holding hands, to Anjola sitting on Azeem's thighs and sharing kisses in dark corners during prep. Anjola is happy and Azeem looks contented.

Scene IV

It is break time. Anjola is writing some notes under a tree. Chiamaka uses her hand to protect her eyes from the sun to see who is sitting by the tree. Chiamaka walks towards Anjola with concerned looks.

Chiamaka: Anjola, what happened? You are writing under the tree with all seriousness. Do not tell me your class notes are incomplete. As you know, people with incomplete notes visit this spot.

Anjola: Hmmm, you got me. I have become a client.

Azeem: (Stunned) Anjola, how is that possible. How can you have spaces in your notes when we are boarders?

Anjola: Chiamaka, please leave that thing.

Chiamaka: I am upset at the level of negligence you exhibit towards your studies. You are not even bothered about the strokes of cane from Miss Dele.

Anjola: I will not receive a stroke of her cane because it is only my Biology note that is not up to date. You know, babe. Biology notes are very long, coupled with the numerous drawings. And I really do not like the subject and its subject teacher.

Chiamaka: (Laughs) Anjola, you had better start liking it, because it is a core subject. (Glance at wristwatch.) I will leave you now. Please, try to complete your note; you do not want the teacher to embarrass you in front of the classroom. Bye, Anjola.

Anjola: Thanks for caring, dear.

Chiamaka: You are welcome, any time. Please, share any difficulty you encounter in Biology. I will be happy to help.

Anjola: (Smiles) Thanks babe.

(Azeem strolls towards the tree spot with a warm smile.)

Azeem: (Waves at Anjola and stops by Chiamaka.) Hey, Chiamaka.

Chiamaka: (Rolls eyes) Oh, I see. So, this is your main purpose of being here.

Anjola:	(Blushes and flips onto the next page.)
Azeem:	(Coughs and winks at Chiamaka.)
Chiamaka:	I will leave the two of you.

(Anjola and Azeem smile at each other.)

(Light fades.)

The school first term ends. Anjola and Azeem bid each other an emotional farewell.

ACT FOUR

Scene I

Green College school premises. Mr Adebayo turns to Anjola.

Mr Adebayo: This is another term and I hope you will do well in your studies. Any flop from you, I am withdrawing you to a local school so that I do not have to worry about the huge sum I pay in this school. Do I make myself clear?

Anjola: (Shudders.)

Mr Adebayo: Anjola, are you suddenly dumb?

Anjola: No, sir.

Mr Adebayo: Well, I know you heard me loud and clear. I pray for wisdom upon you.

Anjola: Thank you, daddy.

Mr Adebayo: (Talks to the driver from the back seat.) Thomas, please, bring Anjola's luggage to her hostel.

Thomas:	Yes sir. (Alight from the car and carries Anjola's luggage.)
Mr Adebayo:	Be successful. Give back in better methods, the knowledge your teachers have imparted in you. You have to do better, I am not happy about your bad performances. Your mother and I have spoken to you. Now, all I can say is a word is enough for the wise. I know you are not foolish. Cut off from every distraction and focus on your education.
Anjola:	Yes sir, I will. Thank you so much, sir.
Mr Adebayo:	(Holds Anjola's head) I know you would make us proud.
Anjola:	(Alights and waves) Bye daddy. (Walks sluggishly to the hostel.)
Thomas:	(Comes out of the hostel) Bye, bye, small madam.
Anjola:	Thanks, Mr Thomas. Goodbye.

(Light fades.)

Light shines upstage. (The housemistress charges into the refectory in annoyance. There is loud murmuring as students scamper to poise.)

Miss Dele: I thought I gave an instruction an hour again. Who are the students to clean downstairs' toilets? (Clap hands.) Come on; speak up my dear boys and girls. Why the sudden silence? Some moments ago, one could mistake this modest dining hall for a party hall or a market square.

Anjola: (Comes through the refectory door) Oh no, the atmosphere is not friendly. (She takes a step backward and briskly turns around.)

Miss Dele: Hey, miss. Where do you think you are going? The last time I checked, you were a student of this renowned school and that means you have to take part in all the activities around here.

Anjola: (Clutches her water bottle and turns around.)

Miss Dele: You will join the others to tidy these mess around here.

Anjola: But ma, my dad just dropped me in school. (Spreads arms and turns around.) How am I a part of this mess?

Miss Dele: Anjola Adebayo! You had better watch your tongue. (Clap hands.) Get to work.

    The students scurry about the hall, cleaning,

sweeping, and dusting.

Anjola: I am so unlucky. (Coughs.) Everywhere is so dusty. I should have resumed a week later.

(Light fades on Anjola, waving off dust from her face.)

(Light shines downstage. Anjola yawns from weariness. She drops her broom and dusts off some pecks of dirt in her hair. From a distance, Anjola sees Azeem and Nkechi holding hands and laughing over each other. Her bosom rises and falls in anger and jealousy. She angrily walks to her hostel.)

(Light fades.)

Scene II

In the dormitory. Anjola is deep in thought while holding her book. Oluchi waves a hand in Anjola's face to get her attention. Oluchi bangs her hand on the bunk and Anjola snaps.

Anjola: (Opens book) Where were we? Oluchi, what is the formula for…

Oluchi: Anjola, will you just stop trying to irritate me. (Angry) Anjola, this is like the third time, I am explaining how the formula works, but you have been completely out of this world. (Drops pen and paper.) I would also like to know what is happening in space. I might be encouraged to be an astronaut.

Anjola: I did not travel to space. It is all in my head, and it burns here. (Touches heart.)

Oluchi: It is burning because you have refused to share what is bothering you. You succeeded in wasting my precious time.

Anjola: I am sorry, Oluchi. Please, let us carry on.

Oluchi: Eh, you and who should carry on? Please, I am exhausted. Light out was an hour ago. Pity me, biko. I want to rest my head. However, I would like to know what have you distracted. You look worried, girl.

Anjola: Hmmm, Oluchi, please do not judge me when you hear it.

Oluchi: I will not. So, come on with it.

Anjola: It is just that. (Inhales and exhales.) Lately, Azeem makes me feel insecure.

Oluchi: (Scratches her eyes and yawns) How do you mean?

Anjola: (Looks offended) I have not begun, you are already bored. Pele, I am sorry for stressing you.

Oluchi: Oh, Anjola, quit beating round the bush. I am sleepy for goodness sake.

Anjola: Well, he is always with Nkechi nowadays. I think something might be going on between them. I do not feel good about it.

Oluchi: Well, I advise you tell him how you feel.

Anjola: Why should I? He should know what he is

doing with Nkechi is not right. Except he is doing it intentionally to hurt me, I guess.

Oluchi: You have many doubts in your mind. If you did not know him to the extent of being honest and trustworthy, why did you accept to be his girlfriend?

Anjola: (Chews bottom lip.)

Oluchi: Anjola tell me the truth, why are you with Azeem.

Anjola: Well, I was actually trying the all-rounder thing; you know, like trying to be perfect with good grades and still have a high social life. And with Azeem by my side, I was getting all the attention. Most girls did everything to get his attention but he came for me.

Oluchi: Well, I really do not know what to say, but what is happening is not a surprise, because you were not genuine and he was probably not transparent as well.

Anjola: If things are getting worse, I will break up with him publicly, so that everyone will know I made the move to dump him. I will not look like the fool or the…

Oluchi:	Wow, you are too much. Is that what has been playing in your little head? Wow, Anjola Adebayo. When will you cease to amaze me? Well, exam is next week, so leave all these unnecessary drama. Azeem did not pay your school fees, so you had better read for you and your parents. Who knows, this guy might be reading now and you are stressing for no good reason.
Anjola:	Let us leave all that. Please, let us continue.
Oluchi:	(Bats eyelashes) Continue with what? (Lies down.) Please, let me sleep. (Covers with a blanket.)
Anjola:	Good night, my dear friend. (Grins and goes to her bunk. Lies down and instantly falls asleep.)

(Blackout.)

Scene III

The next day. The bell clangs to announce break time.

Azeem: (Enters Anjola's class) Hello pretty. (Sits in front of her and waves a hand in her face.) Hello. I hope I am welcomed.

Anjola: (Looks up and raises an eyebrow) What do you want?

Azeem: (Spreads his arms) What do you mean?

Anjola: You just showed up in my face and say 'hi' after four weeks of resumption. I guess you have been blind towards my path.

Azeem: I guess I have not been in your radar as well. You did not bother to say 'hi' to me, you were just waiting for me to make the first move, and here, I am at your feet. (He bows.)

Anjola: (Pouts and looks away.)

Azeem: Come on, pretty. Believe me, Anjola. I wanted to talk to you on Saturday, but after that drama with Miss Dele that day, I figured it was not a good time.

Anjola: (Snorts) How is your girlfriend, Nkechi?

Azeem: Wait, what? I hope you do not have the wrong idea about Nkechi and I? We are just friends.

Anjola: Yeah, right. Just the way you and I, are just friends. (Scoffs.) You cannot fool me. I have seen the way your eyes follow her every move. You should have just appointed yourself her personal bodyguard.

Azeem: Anjola, you have it all wrong. We are just friends, and nothing more. (Crosses heart.)

Anjola: Why should I believe you? (Shakes head.) Boys will be boys. You say it is a neutral friendship. Yet, I did not know how to classify our relationship. That plain relationship with Nkechi made you ignore me to the point you did not reply my text messages during the holiday. You were so active on every group chat, and could not spare a minute thought for me. Boy, you are sadly incredible.

Azeem: (Holds a chair for support) Babe, (Whispers.) Lower your voice. You are beginning to yell and the whole school might think we are at war.

Anjola: Azeem, believe me when I say you cannot handle my wrath. I will win any war against you. Now, leave me in peace.

Azeem: Ah, Anjola, you get angry easily. Let us sheath our swords. I am sorry; I was unaware of my bad behaviour towards you.

Anjola: (Emotional) Azeem, you were so unfair. I was dating myself. I did not know what to say when my friends asked if we were still together. Are we still in a relationship?

Azeem: (Clears throat and holds her hands) Of course, baby. We are. None of us called it a break, right?

Anjola: (Sighs) Azeem, please leave, as you can see, you rudely interrupted my reading. I have a test.

Azeem: So, you really want me to leave.

Anjola: Yes, and ignore me as you have been doing.

Azeem: But I said I am sorry.

Anjola: (Stares intently and rolls eyes) Please leave and do not ever talk to Nkechi again.

Azeem: (Smirks) Anything for you, babe. (Kisses her cheeks.)

Anjola: (Pushes him away) I have a test.

Azeem: Is that to say you forgive me.

Anjola: You cannot imagine what I would do if I see you around Nkechi.

Azeem: Now, I have my answer.

Anjola: And how did you get the answer?

Azeem: I got the response I needed, and it was through your jealous outburst. (Winks.) Thanks baby. (Stands.) Meet me under the tree after school. I will be patiently waiting under our canopy of love.

Anjola: (Rolls eyes and waves him off.)

Azeem and Anjola rekindle their relationship. They enjoy each other's company with brief hugs and kisses, but this lasted for a week.

(Light fades.)

It is club week. Anjola studies in the classroom. Azeem walks in on Anjola.

Azeem: I thought you went for the debate competition.

Anjola: As you can see, I am here.

Azeem: Okay, thanks for supporting me during the basketball competition, you are a darling. (Positions his lips for a kiss.)

Anjola: (Moves away) You did not show up on Saturday. I told you to come and teach me economics' graph and you promised to do that on Friday. Look here, Azeem, I make sacrifices for you while I have a lot to cover. But you do nothing for me.

Azeem: If you are tired of me, tell me so that I can move on.

Anjola: Azeem, just one thing I asked of you and you are behaving this way. This is not fair and I even asked because you made me miss my tutorial with Oluchi.

Azeem: Your complaint is making me feel bad.

Anjola: Okay, I am sorry. But why did you not come on Saturday, what were you doing?

Azeem: Well. (Clears throat and stutters.) I was with Busayo in the Fine Art studio. The truth is, I was on my way to call you, and then she asked me to teach her drawings. (Touches Anjola's cheek.) You know I like drawing, so I jumped at the offer.

Anjola: Azeem, Busayo is not offering Fine Art, it is French.

Azeem: (He shrugs) Well, maybe she is into Fine Art now, who knows.

Anjola: (Laughs) I cannot believe it, you are finally rubbing it on my face. (Holds Azeem's hands and looks into his eyes.) Everyone knows you carry different girls to Fine Art studio; you are just a playboy. (Walks out.)

Azeem: (Smirks.)

(Light fades.)

(In the library. Ewa is reading. Anjola and Oluchi are having a tutorial. Oluchi scribbles some figures and proceeds to solve a question. Anjola focuses on how Oluchi breaks down the problem and arrives at two possible answers.)

Oluchi: (Beams) Just like that, so simple, probability is one of the simplest topics.

Anjola: Thanks, dear.

Oluchi: You are welcome; I was not really expecting you today. It has been long we did this.

Anjola: Yeah, I was a bit busy.

Oluchi: Hmmm, okay.

Anjola: What?

Oluchi: You are going through a lot, and everyone knows it, fix yourself up. You are turning into a complete mess.

Anjola: Oluchi…

Oluchi: Babe, I have to go now, Miss Dele wanted to see me. (Leaves in a hurry.)

Anjola: (Smiles sadly) Am I really a mess? (Pack up books.)

(Lost in deep thoughts, Anjola did not hear Mrs Ezekiel's footsteps.)

Mrs Ezekiel: Anjola.

Anjola: (Shakes head and sighs loudly.)

(Ewa is about to leave the library.)

Ewa: (Touches Anjola's arm) What are you thinking?

Anjola: What?

Ejiro: Mrs Ezekiel is calling you.

Anjola: (Looks up to Mrs Ezekiel) Oh, yes ma.

Mrs Ezekiel: Anjola, what is the matter?

Anjola: (Shakes head vigorously) It is nothing. I am all right, ma.

Mrs Ezekiel: A problem shared is half solved. Have you heard that saying?

Anjola: (Smiles) Ma, it is nothing. I was just recalling what I learnt today.

Mrs Ezekiel: (Smiles knowingly) When I was in Secondary School, I had a big challenge; funny enough, the challenge had no link to school issues.

Anjola: Oh.

Mrs Ezekiel: My dad had lost his job in a public hospital. I told the matron about it, and she paved a way for my dad to get an employment in a private hospital. If I had not told her, I will not be a graduate today.

Anjola: But my dad has a gainful employment. We have not suffered any financial setbacks.

Mrs Ezekiel: (Chuckles) I did not say your parents are jobless. I was just giving an instance of why someone can be moody with my personal experience.

Anjola: Oh. (Clears throat.) Now I get it. My mind travelled far. I am sorry. (Rests hands on her waist.)

Mrs Ezekiel: Are you pregnant?

Anjola: (Stunned) What? How can I be pregnant?

Mrs Ezekiel: It is a reasonable guess because…

Anjola: Ma, I am not. I am going through a rough phase, that's all.

Mrs Ezekiel: I have gone through every phase; you have gone through and are going through. Anjola, you are not alone. Many boys and girls like you are facing the same challenges. That is why I am talking to you. If I can help you get through this, you can also reach out to others.

Anjola: Ma, you know my academic performances are having a reset and I am flopping at the chances of getting it right.

Mrs Ezekiel: (Nods) And why is that?

Anjola: Well, I think I made a mistake or I think I overdid the getting notorious thing. I could not stand everyone looking down on me. It was unbearable.

Mrs Ezekiel:	Who are the people that look down on you?
Anjola:	My classmates, those in the same hostel with me, the teaching and non-teaching staffs.
Mrs Ezekiel:	(Grins) Is that all? I am surprised you did not include the external examination board. (Shakes head.) It is all in your head. Anjola, I could say that half of the school does not know you. So, why do you think 'everyone' is looking down on you. Tell me something serious.
Anjola:	No ma, I am actually serious, if you are not popular, nobody respects you.
Mrs Ezekiel:	What kind of respect?
Anjola:	Like nobody tries to ride over you, junior students are scared of you; senior students dot on you, being notorious and mischievous in school is cool.
Mrs Ezekiel:	Really. (Laughs) So, this is your actual distraction. Tell me the benefit of this popularity.
Anjola:	I really do not know. You will be the centre of discussion. Your name will be on everybody's lips.
Mrs Ezekiel:	And all will base on frivolities, right?

Anjola: (Wriggles hands.)

Mrs Ezekiel: This popularity you are craving is useless, it will not make you successful, and it would not give you A(s). Anjolaoluwa, if you want popularity, ace your examination and WAEC. Win gold medals in competitions, those kinds of popularity fetch you purposeful recognition and many opportunities in life, not boys and some dumb presence you are looking for.

Anjola: (Looks surprised.)

Mrs Ezekiel: I hope I am making some sense. You have less than three years in the school, and you have to make it count positively. If you have other skills, you could make use of the extra-curriculum time to practice.

Anjola: (Eyes brightens.)

Mrs Ezekiel: No one looks down on someone who is maximising his or her time towards excellence. And you, Anjola, do not know what to do with time, and you also fail to recognize your purpose, hence people will look down on you.

Anjola: (Bows) But, I have been trying my best.

Mrs Ezekiel: But your best has not been good enough.

Anjola:	(Raise questioning eyes to Mrs Ezekiel.)
Mrs Ezekiel:	Yes, I am saying the truth. Okay, tell me. When last did they announce your name on the assembly ground for wining a competition? When did the school announce your name for any award or positive deed?
Anjola:	(Shoulders drop) Yes, you are right.
Mrs Ezekiel:	So, please take a bold step, cut off from every distraction, and maximize your stay in Green College. The ball is in your court; you can play it towards the goal post for a win or lose, but bear in mind that only you will face the consequences of your actions.
Anjola:	Thank you so much, ma. I feel much better. It feels like God sent you to me.
Mrs Ezekiel:	(Smiles) It is wonderful to hear that.
Anjola:	Thank you, ma.

Anjola and Mrs Ezekiel hug each other.

(Light fades.)

ACT FIVE

Scene I

In the hostel. Chiamaka polishes her shoes to perfection. Anjola envies the gleaming shoes and winks.

Anjola: (Turns lazily to Chiamaka) Please, I am tired, help me shine my shoes. (Grins impishly.)

Chiamaka: How much will you pay me?

Anjola: Chai, you are a real Igbo girl! You like money a lot, just apply small polish on my shoes.

Oluchi: (Laughs and rolls on her bed.) Anjola, let us get ready.

Anjola: Yes, Oluchi. We are getting late. I will get my bag. (Gets off the bed.)

(Chiamaka sees Peju from the window. Peju comes into the dormitory with a gift bag.)

Chiamaka: Peju, is it your birthday?

Peju: (Drops it on Anjola's bed) It is for Anjola.

There is sudden silence in the dormitory. Everyone clusters around Anjola.

Peju: (Winks at Anjola) It is from Azeem.

Barakat: (Reads the letters on the card) Hmmm, all these just to tender an apology.

Ewa: Oh, yes. When you are big, you are big.

Peju: Look, girls. He bought her a top and skirt.

Chiamka: Eh, Anjola, I could wear the snickers.

                     (Anjola is oblivious to the chatters going on around her.)

Anjola: (In an aside) What should I do? I have already crossed my mind to begin a new path in life. (Takes a deep breath.) No more distractions. (Sighs wearily.) But see how everyone is crowding me now. Oh, Anjola. (Paces and softly hits her head with both hands.) What to do? (Scratches head and exhales.) This popularity is not worth it.

Peju: Anjola say something.

Anjola: (Stops pacing and frowns) Tell Azeem that I do not appreciate his gifts. He has broken the school's law. I am sure he sneaked these items into the school on resumption or he asked one of the day students to get them. (Drops the gift bag on the floor.)

Peju: (Whistles softly) Girl, are you for real?

Anjola: Yes, I am tired of him. He is boring and he does not add any value or worth to my life, whoever wants him should go ahead and have all of him. I do not care.

Barakat: (Snorts and bats eyelashes) It is now you realise it. Eya... You are dumber than an imbecile is.

Anjola: I know you have a sly tongue, which is why I will not pay heed to your malicious words.

Barakat: So much guts. Come, are you really done with him.

Anjola: Yes, and I have made up my mind, so any bigmouth should go ahead and broadcast this little info. I do not give a damn. Read my lips. (Traces lower lips with a finger.) I do not give a damn.

Barakat: (Laughs mockingly) This is serious.

Anjola: (Looks intensely at Barakat and sighs) Oluchi.

Oluchi:	Yes, Anjola.
Anjola:	It is time for Biology tutorial.
Oluchi:	Shall we.
Anjola:	Yes, I believe we shall. (Stands purposefully and beams with an aggressive determination to succeed.)

(Anjola and Oluchi leave for the courtyard.)

(Light fades.)

Scene II

The term ends with Green College's Prize Giving Day. There is flurry of activities. From backstage, students change from their school uniforms into different costumes. Various groups exhibit performances that thrill the audience. There is drama, music, dance, indoor sports, and other fun games. The students change into uniforms immediately after a performance and move downstage to join the audience.

Mrs Olufemi: (Mounts the podium) Distinguished guests, esteemed parents, guardians, our excellent teachers and indomitable students, it is with utmost pleasure I usher you into the next segment of our program. Right now, we will call on the awardees. (Bobs.) And my co-anchor is no other than Mr Oyeniyi.

Audience: (Cheers.)

Mrs Olufemi: It is always fun to do this. So, let us get the names rolling. We will begin with the SS 1

	Awards. Best in Biology.
Mr Oyeniyi:	Anjola Adebayo
Mrs Oulfemi:	Best in English Language
Mr Oyeniyi:	Anjola Adebayo
Mrs Olufemi:	Best in Physics
Mr Oyeniyi:	Anjola Adebayo, please come forward to receive your awards.
Anjola:	(Walks cheerfully with teary eyes, collect her awards and whispers into Mrs Olufemi's ear.)
Audience:	(Claps continuously…)
Mrs Olufemi:	(Puts the Mic aside) Okay, it seems Miss Anjola Adebayo has something to say (Gives microphone to Anjola and steps aside.)
Anjola:	Philippians 4: 13 says with God, all things are Possible. You cannot achieve anything on earth, if there is no will and determination in working towards it. To have will and determination is one thing but to focus is another? My will and determination in the past was becoming the most popular girl amongst my peers. It ended up in premium tears.
Audience:	(Laughs.)

Anjola: I am grateful to my parents for the stern encouragements they gave to me. I cherish their love and support. One of my biggest motivators is Mrs Ezekiel. God sent her into my life at the ripened time. If not for her interference and guidance, I would not be standing here.

Mrs Ezekiel: (Flushes as all eyes are on her) Oh, my world.

Anjola: She redirected my steps to the right path. God bless you ma, for not abandoning me and still believing in me.

Mrs Ezekiel: (Smiles and place hands on bosom.)

Anjola: And to my friends, especially Oluchi, I am grateful for all the help you gave to me. Your selfless coaching really fine-tuned my academics in positive ways. Thank you.

Oluchi: (Bows and mouths) Thank you…

Anjola: I never saw myself, collecting an award throughout my stay in school, but here I am today. (Sniffs and holds up her awards.) Cheers to hard work, diligence and resilience.

Audience: (Cheers and claps.)

Anjola:	I just want to tell my junior students that, distractions will surely come in secondary school but you can always overcome them by constantly reawakening your focus. Do not seek validations from every person. You may not know who is out to exploit your foolishness and take advantage of your low self-esteem.
Barakat:	(Snorts and stares at Anjola's awards with hate) Who does she think she is. (She waves a hand across her face.) Duh.
Anjola:	We all know the difference between good and evil. So, let us walk and work according to good ethics. Thank you. (Leaves podium.)
Audience:	(Gives Anjola a standing ovation.)
	(Anjola returns to her seat. She receives hugs and pecks from her parents. She holds her breath and gives a moment of respect to Eniola Ajayi.)
Anjola:	Eni, this is for you. (Kisses the awards.)
	(Students, parents and staffs of Green College exchange pleasantries.)

Oluwafunmilayo Inemesit Adewole

(Blackout.)

www.ingramcontent.com/pod-product-compliance
Lightning Source LLC
Chambersburg PA
CBHW052258150726
48001CB00024B/1925